a

b

c

d

An Alphabet
Book of
Cats and
Dogs

by Sheila Moxley

Megan Tingley Books

 Little, Brown and Company
Boston New York London

For Rick
and Cricklewood

Aa

Arnold is an amazing aviator.

Bb

Beatrice balances beautifully
on her ball.

Cc

Carlos wears a checkered
cap in his convertible.

Dd
Deborah delivers doughnuts
door-to-door.

Ee

Edward enjoys eating eggs.

Ff

Gg
Ginger grows geraniums
in her garden.

Hh

Henrietta has her hat on.

Ii

Ivan is gliding on ice.

Jj

Joe jumps and jives to his

Kk

Ll

Louise longs for letters from her love.

Mm

Ming masters a magic trick.

Nn

Ned's new necktie is neat.

Oo

Oswald often orders orange

Pp

Patrick paints pet portraits
with his paw.

Qq

Quentin curls up quietly on his quilt.

Rr

Renée races around in her
rocket ship.

Ss

Sam sails the seas on sunny days

Tt

Tabitha taps her tambourine with perfect timing.

Uu

Ursula stays underneath her umbrella.

Vv

Victoria buys a violin on
vacation in Venice.

MAY
M T W Th F S S
1 2 3 4 5
6 7 8 9 10 11 12
13 14 15 16 17 18 19
20 21 22 23 24 25 26
27 28 29 30 31

Ww

Wendy wears weird wigs on Wednesdays.

Xx

Xavier is an excellent
xylophone player.

Yy

Yolanda yearns for a yellow yo-yo.

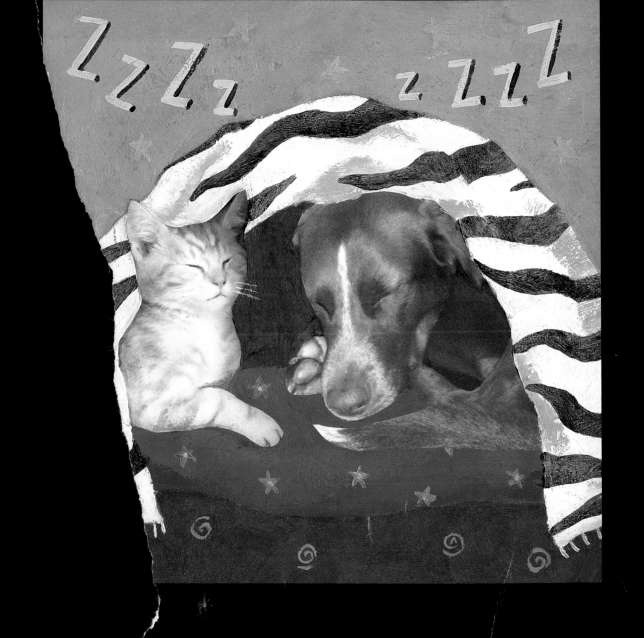

Zack and Zelda like to nap in their zebra-striped blanket . . .
ZzZzZzZzZzZzZzZzZz.

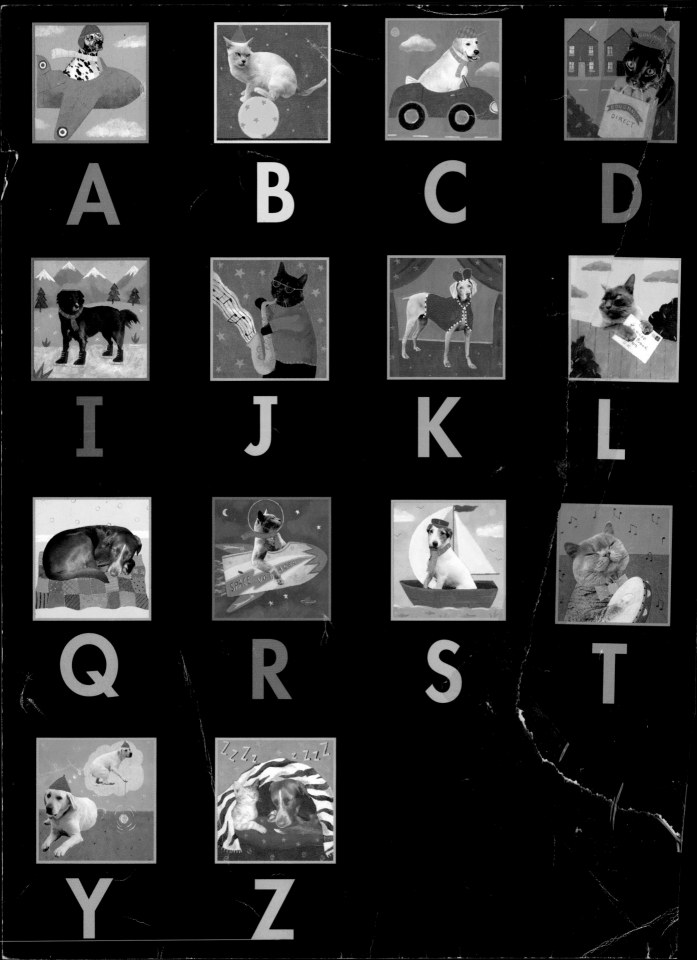

E F G H

M N O P

U V W X

A note about the artwork in this book:

No computers were used in the creation of the art —
although this could change as soon as I become com-
puter-literate! For now, there's no substitute for some
old-fashioned painting and a bit of cutting and sticking
with a scalpel and some sticky-tape. Most important, I
had a plentiful supply of photos so I'd like to thank all
the cats and dogs who cooperated and allowed me
to take their pictures. In fact, I'd even like to thank the
ones who didn't cooperate and hid behind the sofa,
or zoomed up the nearest tree as soon as I got my
camera out!

—S. M.